THIS WALKER BOOK BELONGS TO:

For John and Katya Ivie, two winners ~ R. W.

For Max ~ A. R.

First published 2002 by Walker Books Ltd
87 Vauxhall Walk, London SE11 5HJ

This edition published 2003

10 9 8 7 6 5 4 3

Text © 2002 Rick Walton
Illustrations © 2002 Arthur Robins

The right of Rick Walton and Arthur Robins to be identified as
author and illustrator respectively of this work has been asserted by
them in accordance with the Copyright, Designs and Patents Act 1988

This book has been typeset in Klepto ITC

Printed in China

British Library Cataloguing in Publication Data: a catalogue record
for this book is available from the British Library

ISBN 0-7445-8018-8

www.walkerbooks.co.uk

BERTIE WAS A WATCHDOG

WATCHDOG

illustrated by

Rick Walton

Arthur Robins

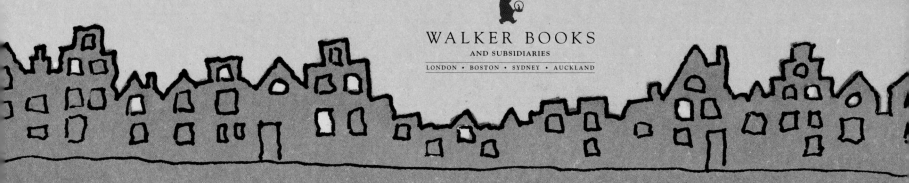

WALKER BOOKS
AND SUBSIDIARIES
LONDON · BOSTON · SYDNEY · AUCKLAND

Bertie

was a watchdog.

But Bertie wasn't called
a watchdog because
he was big, or mean,
or scary.

He was called a watchdog

because he was about the size

of a watch.

Bertie was a **very** small dog.

So when a horrible robber
came into the house,
late one night,
and saw
Bertie . . .

"Ha, ha! What a tiny dog!" said the robber. "I'm not afraid of you."

"Why not?" said Bertie.

"Because you probably bite like a fly!" said the robber.

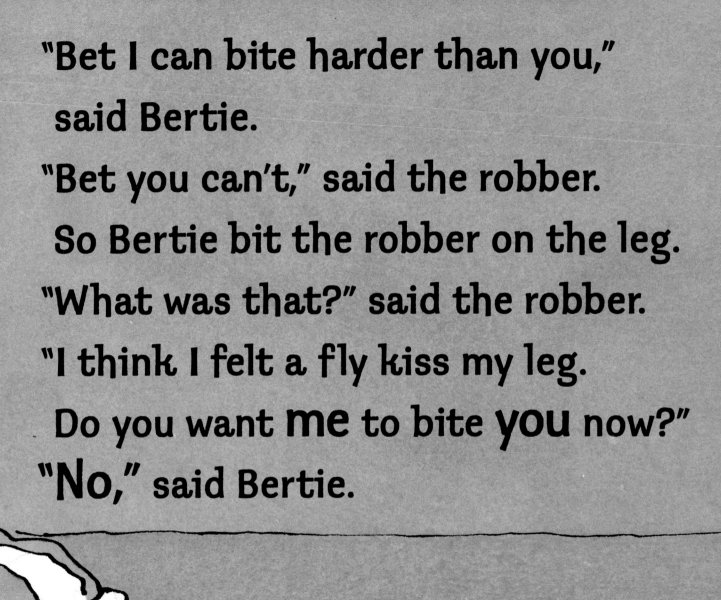

"Bet I can bite harder than you," said Bertie.

"Bet you can't," said the robber.

So Bertie bit the robber on the leg.

"What was that?" said the robber.

"I think I felt a fly kiss my leg. Do you want **me** to bite **you** now?"

"**No,**" said Bertie.

But the robber bit Bertie anyway.

"Yeow!"
said Bertie.
"Ha!" said
the robber.
"I win!"

"Bet I can chase you and catch you," said Bertie.
"Bet you can't," said the robber.

Bertie chased the robber around the sofa.

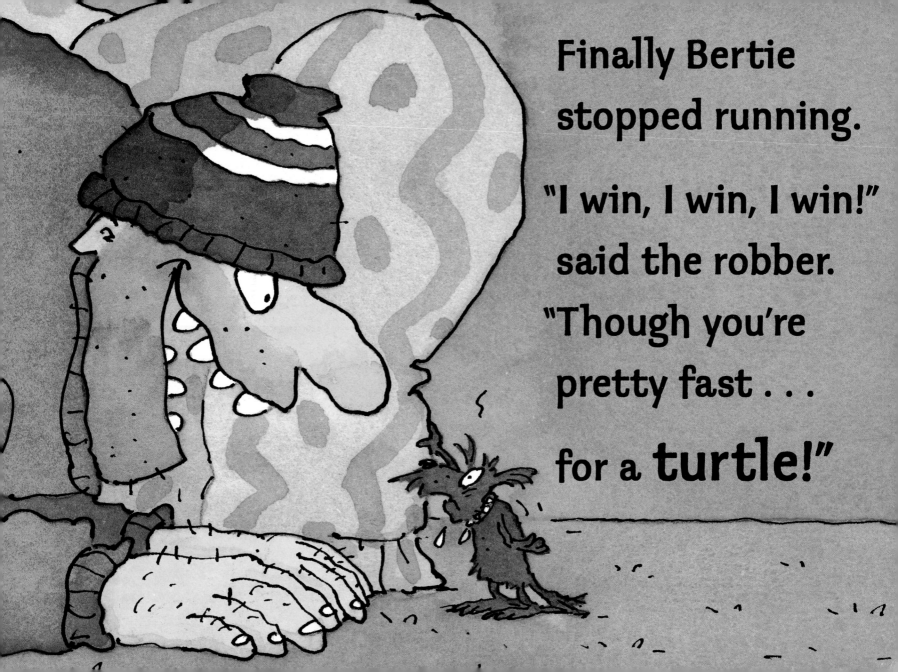

Finally Bertie stopped running.

"I win, I win, I win!" said the robber. "Though you're pretty fast . . .

for a **turtle!**"

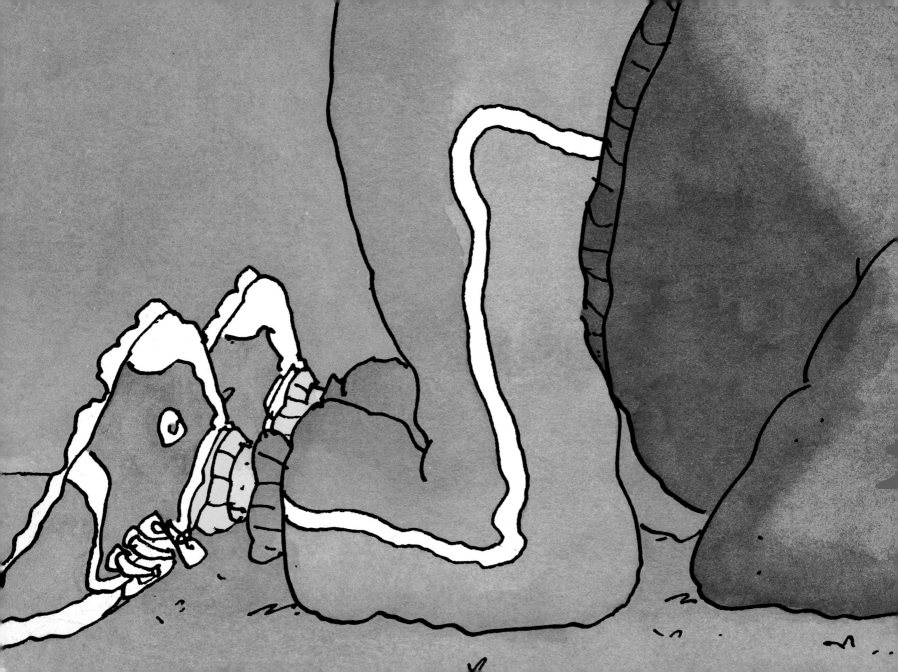

eeep!

barked Bertie.

HA HA HA!

HA!

HA!

A HA

"HA HA HA! Just as
I thought," said the robber.
"You're not a dog, you're
a **mouse**! Let me show
you how a **real** dog barks."

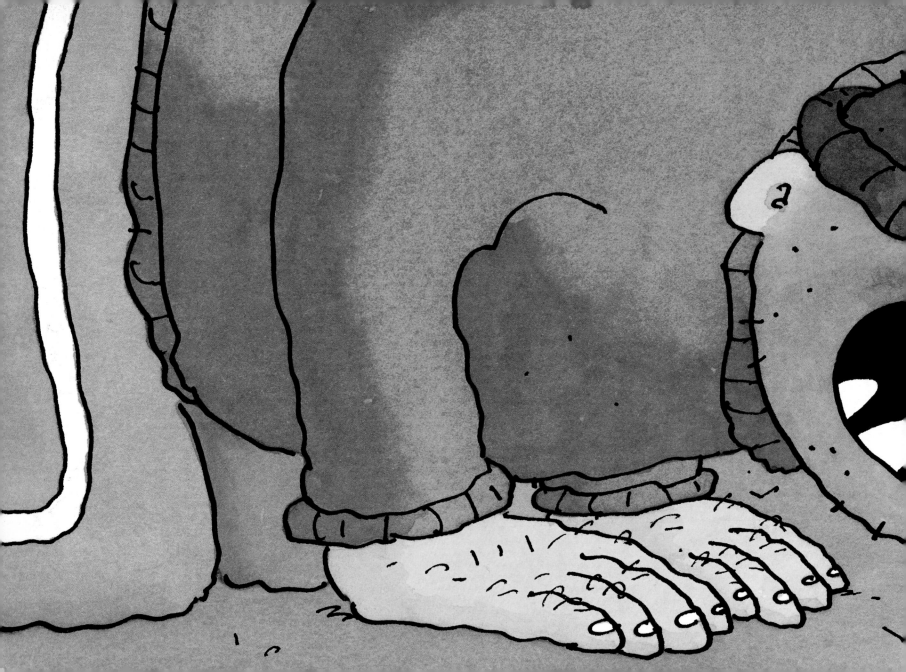

And the robber took a deep breath, bared his teeth, and shouted . . . .

"Is that as loud as you can bark?" said Bertie.

"You don't think that was loud?" said the robber. "Well, listen to **this** . . ."

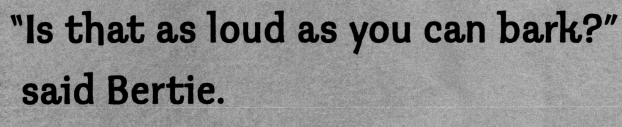

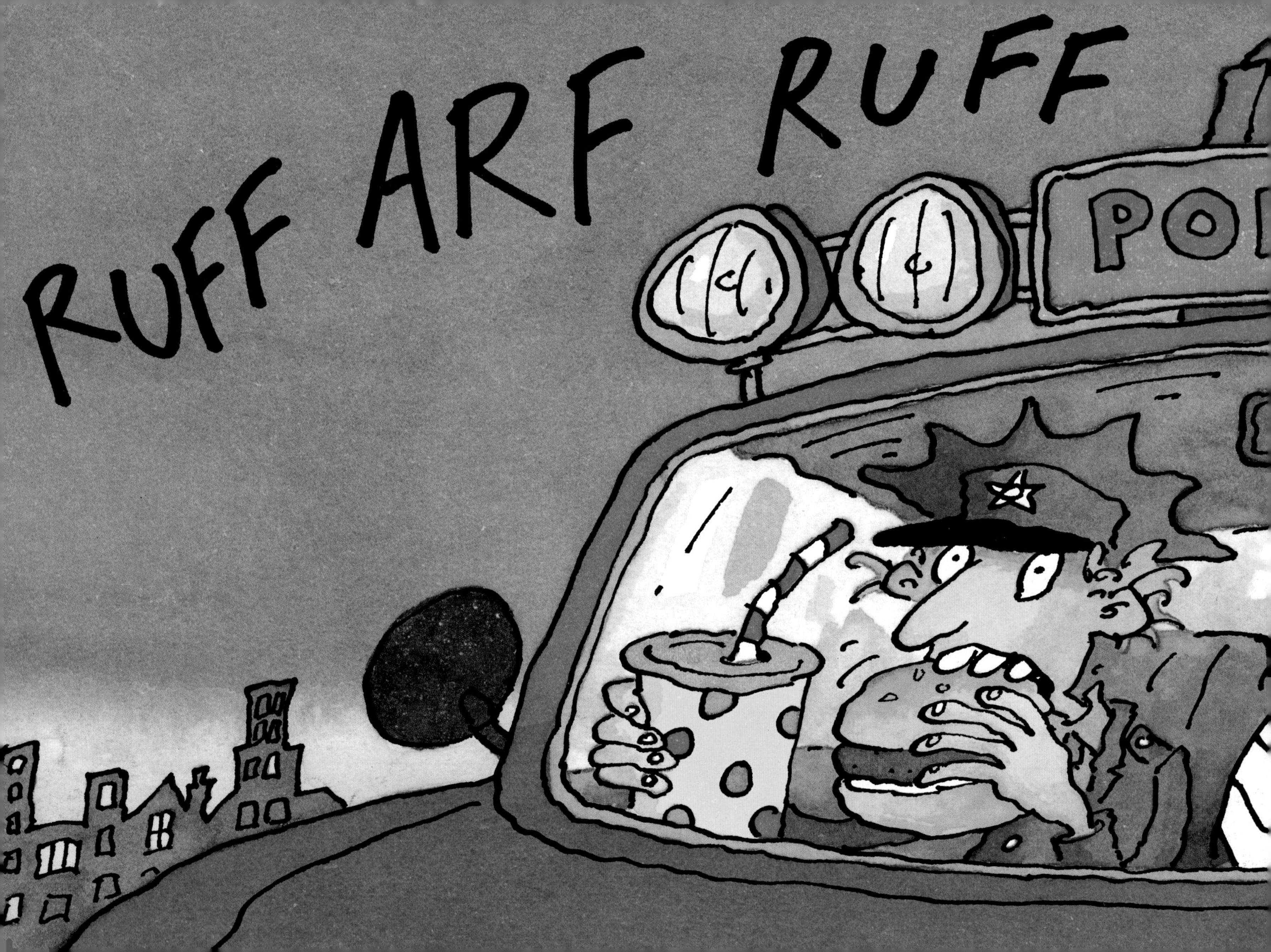
RUFF ARF RUFF

Just then the door flew open.
It was the **POLICE!**

"It's him!"
they shouted,
and they chased
the robber
around the
sofa . . .

and caught him,
and handcuffed him.

"We heard your barking, little dog," the sergeant said, "and came to investigate. We've been looking for this robber for a long time. You're a **hero!**"

Bertie grinned
at the robber
and said . . .

WALKER BOOKS is the world's leading independent publisher of children's books. Working with the best authors and illustrators we create books for all ages, from babies to teenagers – books your child will grow up with and always remember. So…

FOR THE BEST CHILDREN'S BOOKS, LOOK FOR THE BEAR